FAR OUT
CLASSIC STORIES

STONE ARCH BOOKS
a capstone imprint

INTRODUCING...

BLINKER NUB

PETER PAN

THE DUST BOYS

CAPTAIN HOOK

WENDY DARLING

JOHN AND MICHAEL DARLING

in...

Far Out Classic Stories is published by
Stone Arch Books,
an imprint of Capstone.
1710 Roe Crest Drive
North Mankato, Minnesota 56003
www.capstonepub.com

Library of Congress Cataloging-in-
Publication Data is available on the
Library of Congress website.
ISBN: 978-1-4965-8686-5 (hardcover)
ISBN: 978-1-4965-9193-7 (paperback)
ISBN: 978-1-4965-8687-2 (eBook PDF)

Summary: A boy named Peter Pan ran
off to a magically spooky place to
become . . . a mummy! After overhearing
Wendy Darling telling her brothers scary
stories, Peter brings them all to Mummy
Land too. But the island is filled with lots
of creepy creatures, including a skeleton
pirate who wants to put Peter in the
tomb once and for all!

Designed by Hilary Wacholz
Edited by Abby Huff
Lettered by Jaymes Reed

Printed and bound in the USA.
PA99

FAR OUT CLASSIC STORIES

PETER PAN IN MUMMY LAND

A GRAPHIC NOVEL

BY BENJAMIN HARPER

ILLUSTRATED BY FERN CANO

One night, Peter came to the home of the Darling family. He was going to scare the kids!

The twins heard footsteps coming up the stairs. *CLOMP! CLOMP! CLOMP!*

Then what happened?

But he got caught up in Wendy's amazing ghost story.

Then . . . Hey, who are you?!

It's a mummy! Just like in your story!

SNAG!

Peter flew away. But there was one problem . . .

Hey, mummy, you're unraveling!

Well if that wasn't the strangest thing. A *flying mummy!*

I hope he comes back. Mummies are the coolest.

Come live with me in *Mummy Land!* You would love my friends, and they would love your stories.

Your *friends?*

"The Dust Boys. They're like me—they were sick of kid stuff. So I brought them to Mummy Land."

Hmm . . . would I have to be a mummy too?

Nope. But I can teach you how to fly. Plus, my home is full of spooky things that can inspire your stories.

OK, I'll go! But only if my brothers can come too.

Yawn . . . Hey, it's that mummy.

You've got a deal!

YAAAAY!

COOL!

Wait a minute. We already have a master ghost storyteller— ME!

Sorry, Wendy. That's Blinker Nub. She's a magical will-o'-the-wisp. She's usually in charge of story time.

Well hi, Blinker! I'm sure there's room for two storytellers!

Hmph!

OK, are you all ready? Here's what you do to fly...

We're not even real mummies. See?

We just pretend with Peter because being a kid seemed like baby stuff.

You'll all grow up soon enough. You should enjoy being kids while you can!

I say we fly back home.

You can see your parents, and we can still hang out! We can all be friends there too.

YEAH!

But what about Peter?

Wendy began her most terrifying tale.

Denise was walking home from the school dance when she took a wrong turn and ended up in ...

THE GRAVEYARD.

Oh no. Not this one!

Everyone sat silently as they listened to Wendy's words.

Until ...

When Denise opened the coffin, she saw someone lying inside. That someone was . . . HERSELF!

GASP!

I have a feeling things are going to be different around Mummy Land from now on.

The children said goodbye to Peter Pan and Mummy Land.

Liftoff!

And everyone, including Peter, had fun being a kid!

ALL ABOUT THE ORIGINAL STORY!

The character of
Peter Pan was created by
Scottish writer J.M. Barrie.
In 1904 Barrie published a play called
Peter Pan; or, The Boy Who Would Not Grow Up.
A few years later he wrote a novel called *Peter and Wendy.*

In the original, Peter Pan doesn't want to be old—instead he
never wants to grow up! So he leaves home and goes to a
magical place called Neverland where he will never age. There he
lives with a fairy named Tinker Bell and the Lost Boys, kids who
also ran away to keep from growing up.

Peter often visits the home of the Darlings. He loves to listen to
the bedtime stories that Mrs. Darling tells to Wendy, John, and
Michael. One night, Peter forgets his shadow at their house. When
he comes back for it, Wendy spots Peter and helps him put the
shadow back on. Peter is so impressed that he invites Wendy and
her brothers to Neverland. He teaches them to fly and off they go.

The Darlings have many adventures on the island of Neverland with
Peter, Tinker Bell, and the Lost Boys. But eventually they want to
return home to their parents, and the Lost Boys decide to come
with them. Peter, however, refuses to leave.

As the group heads out, a fierce pirate named Captain Hook
captures them! He's called Hook because his hand was eaten by
a crocodile, and he wears a hook in its place. He blames Peter
for the injury and wants to hurt the boy back. Peter rushes
to the pirate ship after learning about Hook's plans. Peter
defeats his foe in a sword fight and rescues his friends.
The Darlings and Lost Boys can now safely
fly back home. Peter still stays
behind, but he promises to
visit them every spring.

A FAR OUT GUIDE TO THE STORY'S MUMMIFIED TWISTS

In the original, Peter Pan is a boy who wants to be young forever. In this version, he's a mummy boy who wants to be old!

Peter's small flying friend is a fairy in the novel. Here she's a will-o'-the-wisp.

The original lagoon had mermaids swimming in its water. This one has plesiosaurs!

Instead of Wendy's mother telling bedtime stories, Wendy is telling ghost stories. And her terrifying tale saves the day!

VISUAL QUESTIONS

Wendy tells really scary stories. How does the art here help add to the spookiness?

1

What's in these thought bubbles, and why are there red Xs through them? Describe how it connects with what Peter is saying.

Look at these panels from page 25. How do you think Peter feels about the Darlings and Dust Boys' decision to leave Mummy Land? What makes you think that?

Why does Captain Hook's dialogue look different from the kids' dialogue? How would you say it if you were reading out loud? Flip back through the story and find other examples of special dialogue text.

AUTHOR

Benjamin Harper has worked as an editor at Lucasfilm LTD. and DC Comics. He currently lives in Los Angeles where he writes, watches monster movies, and hangs out with his cat, Edith Bouvier Beale, III. His other books include the Bug Girl series, *Obsessed with Star Wars*, *Rolling with BB-8*, and *Hansel & Gretel & Zombies*.

ILLUSTRATOR

Fern Cano is an illustrator born in Mexico City, Mexico. He currently resides in Monterrey, Mexico, where he makes a living as an illustrator and colorist. He has done work for Marvel, DC Comics, and role-playing games like Pathfinder from Paizo Publishing. In his spare time, he enjoys hanging out with friends, singing, rowing, and drawing!

GLOSSARY

bandage (BAN-dij)—a strip of cloth used to cover and protect parts of the body

double-crosser (DUH-buhl-KROS-uhr)—a person who cheats others by saying they will do one thing but then doing another

glide (GLAHYD)—to move in a smooth way

gloomy (GLOO-mee)—causing feelings of sadness

horde (HOHRD)—a large group of something (like zombies!)

lagoon (luh-GOON)—a small body of water between the shore and a coral reef

moan (MOHN)—to make a long, low sound, usually in pain or sadness

mummy (MUH-mee)—a dead body that has been kept from breaking down through the use of special salts and has been wrapped in bandages

terrifying (TER-uh-fahy-ing)—causing a great amount of fear

tomb (TOOM)—a room or building that holds dead bodies

unravel (uhn-RAV-uhl)—to come apart bit by bit

will-o'-the-wisp (wil-oh-thuh-WISP)—in folktales, a spirit that appears at night, often in wetlands, as a small light and tries to trick people into getting lost

OLD FAVORITES. NEW SPINS.

FAR OUT CLASSIC STORIES